The Piano Tuner's Wife

by

Jean Yamasaki Toyama

Aignos Publishing
Honolulu, Hawaii
2013

Aignos Publishing, Inc.
1910 Ala Moana Blvd, #20A
Honolulu, HI 96815
www.aignospublishing.com

Printed in the USA

Zachary M. Oliver, editor and publisher
Cover art provided by Donna Lester
Typesetting and Design by Rowen Tabusa
Design by Liang-Han "Kevin" Yu

13-digit ISBN: 978-0-9895191-0-6
10-digit ISBN: 0989519104

This book is mainly fiction based on the author's imagination and the points of departure provided by being the piano tuner's driver.

Honolulu, Hawaii
2013

Other works featured with permission from *Bamboo Ridge Press*

"The Ant Massacre," Issue 100, *Bamboo Ridge* (Fall, 2011)

"Bloody Easy," Issue 100, *Bamboo Ridge* (Fall, 2011)

"Uncle's," Issue 98, *Bamboo Ridge* (Fall, 2010).

"Aproru Pansu," "Seven-year Memorial," "Hair and Smoke" in *Bamboo Ridge* (Fall, 2001)

To Dennis, my tuner
To Mom from where I came

Table of Contents

The Piano Tuner's Wife

Stillborn Stories

The Piano Tuner's Wife

The Prodigy

The nine-foot Steinway concert grand sits right there in the living room with its own designated electric socket built into the floor under it. Not many homes have such a set up, but this is the old Manoa, the Manoa Road Manoa, near where Jackson College once stood. Here the old moneyed homes have high ceilings inside and columned fronts and old world stucco surfaces outside. Some even have lava rock walls with gates and half-circle driveways that lead to a porte cochere. Old money. I look around and try to suppress a *schadenfreude* smile. The house looks like it's lost its money; it could use a new paint job and a gardener, too.

The Manoa rains nourishing lush vegetation that obscure the French windows have also badly affected the Steinway. In spite of the special electric socket the damp chaser has not prevented the strings from rusting. In fact a few in the upper register have snapped and raising the pitch could cause other breaks. Without a restringing, the tuning would need to sit below the standard pitch of A440. But that's not all. More serious is the frozen action. Pound the ivory keys as hard as you like, the hammers rise without strength only to sit mid-air without effect. It's apparent that for many years no music has emerged from this once beautiful instrument. Its glory days are over. That is the verdict of the piano tuner, as Glenda, the owner, listens with her head hanging down at an angle. As if to prove his point, the piano tuner fingers out an arpeggio, and nothing happens.

In that brief silence I remember my envy of rich people, my classmates with big houses, fancy cars. I remember my childhood playmate, Sally, who stopped being my friend because she went to Punahou, and I went off to Stevenson Intermediate School. But now I couldn't envy Glenda. She looks like a scrawny scarecrow, with the beginnings of a dowager hump but only on the left-side. Poor lopsided mini-Quasimodo. Glenda limps. And she has a curious lisp; her sibilants pass through her teeth like a breeze. Rich people are not supposed to have flaws. Oh, yes, lost riches.

Mold grows on the underside of the lid of the aging grand. An ugly grey stain spreads over the once lustrous Santo Domingo mahogany, crown prince of all woods. The dark grains that once rippled like luminous satin, now dull… an old dust rag. "Oh, you can polish this," I tell her, when Glenda asks about the surface. Glenda, can't afford to have the restringing done; she just wants the keys to play and the broken strings replaced.

Once this decision is made, the tuner starts his enormous task, and Glenda retreats to another room. I just look around; it will be a long day. There's mold even on the koa frame enclosing a yellowing page from the *Honolulu Advertiser*. You can smell the years. In the accompanying picture, I can almost recognize the young girl seated at a stunning piano. The article describes a symphony concert where a local youngster of exceptional talent reminded the writer of a young Van Cliburn. That name is familiar. The article discusses her Chinese background. Do more, do better. "Here is a local prodigy with so much promise; we'll hear about her in the future."

"So, you found my fifteen minutes of fame, have you?" Glenda asks as she enters the sunroom carrying some lemonade. "I never bothered to take it down; should though. It collects dust." Glenda's *dust* gently breezes through her teeth.

"I hope you don't mind," I reply aware of my nosey nature. "I was just looking around. People's houses are interesting, don't you think?"

"Interesting? Maybe," she replies, about to feed my curiosity. "My father, he was proud. He's in a home now, Alzheimer's. Lucky for him. My mother died long ago. Lucky for her. That's the whole story. Really." She leaves me sipping my lemonade.

The room is filled with different kinds of artwork along with Glenda memorabilia. A Miro print, *Mujer*, it says. The figure, a rectangular head with a conical body, displays prominent indentations where the heart and the belly should be. It hangs over the mantle by the fireplace. Intriguing, too cliché, maybe.

On the mantle sits a photo of Glenda in a white gown, holding a trophy, an Italian-styled loving cup, probably of sparkling gold plate. But the shine doesn't show in the black and white image. She is standing next to the proud piano. A smiling, pretty girl.

No doubt she was the envy of those who struggled with right-left hand coordination. Too many notes for too few fingers, too many hours of practice, too many demands to be a prodigy. What a burden!

"It must have been hard to have so much expected of you," I whisper to myself.

"You couldn't understand the half of it," Glenda replies out of the blue. Startled I bite my mouth shut. She twists her smile into a knowing smirk, and I feel that she has exacted her revenge for my curiosity.

Glenda returned to Hawai'i after a lifetime in New York City and a divorce. Though she must be in her early fifties or late sixties, she looks much older. There is little left of the girl in the picture who looked perfectly healthy in high school. Glenda says she's disabled now and looks it. She doesn't tell me what happened after Julliard, only that her ex-husband still lives in New York City.

Before she could tell me more, the piano tuner interrupts, "Well, Glenda, at least it plays in tune and no more broken strings."

"Good. I'm going to sell it," she says in a flat voice.

The Devil Chaser

I felt Mrs. Urabe's eyes boring through the back of my head as I took my laptop out of the bag. She was a petite Japanese woman with that tight perm from the 40s. She was an older version of me. Appearing like anybody's aunt, someone you'd forget you ever met except for the smell of old newspapers that lingered around her, she hovered around the loveseat where I was sitting, waiting, perhaps, for an invitation to join me.

She lifted the doilies off the back of my loveseat and peered under them as if she had found some stain that needed attention. I knew she was just looking over my back. It seemed like the temperature was rising, and the newspaper smell turned slightly smokey. This feeling was in contradiction to the ordinariness of this apartment, the banality of her look. She just stood there watching with great interest, while I waited for my old Mac to rev up. I didn't want to be rude, not to a client, but I was excited about a story that had come to me in the middle of the night. I needed to get it down, before the inclination evaporated. It was about a homeless man who buys a winning lottery ticket with his last five bucks, but instead of being happy he feels afraid. I needed to find out why. I hoped that Mrs. Urabe would let me.

I thought my silence would discourage conversation. It didn't. Just as my fingers started flying over the keys, she shot out from behind me, "What you doing?"

"Writing."

"About what?" She moved beside me and peered at the screen.

"A dream I had. I really need to get it down." I tried not to sound impolite.

"The Lottery," she said reading my title. "Didn't Borges already write that one?"

I was surprised, I wouldn't have thought that someone her age would know Borges.

Before I could make a comment, Mrs. Urabe had wiggled into the other half of the loveseat. She smiled at me and said, "I'm so happy to meet a writer. I've been looking for someone to write my stories. Would you listen to see if you'd like to be my writer?"

Why don't you write your own stories, I thought, but before I could refuse, she nodded affirmatively and started to talk. By this time the lottery had evaporated. I felt the pressure of my jaws locking and my lips spreading into a smile despite myself. Her gaze bore into mine.

"When I was thirteen, I suffered from a very high fever," she said lifting her right hand across her forehead and moving it down her face, which suddenly took on the allure of a younger person. "It baffled the doctors. I had no infection, but blisters appeared in my mouth." She opened her mouth and pointed at her inner cheeks. "My mother had to suck them out."

Upon hearing this unnerving detail, my lips sagged open, and my breathing quickened.

"I worried my parents. Finally, my father took me to the *obôsan*, the priest at my mother's Shingon temple."

Obôsan, the word clicked in my head. I remembered my grandmother talking to me about her *obôsan* and how he could heal people in the sugar mill camp. I never gave it much thought until now.

Mrs. Urabe continued to speak, "My mother attended the temple but not my father; he was an individualist, a man of science—a modern man. But in desperation, he went. The *obôsan* had us sit on the floor behind him, while he sprinkled incense on the lighted *senko* before the altar. As the smoke started rising, he chanted. Then he turned around and pointed at me.

'She is possessed.'"

"Me, possessed?" Mrs. Urabe struck her breast as she repeated, "I was possessed." Her voice lowered and she continued as if in a trance. "The *obôsan* explained, 'Two spirits, one living and one dead, have taken possession of her body. In Okinawa, a group of boys tormented a woman. To escape, her spirit entered your daughter's body. Yes, it crossed the ocean. The dead spirit of one of her ancestors is keeping her spirit company to help bring her back to Okinawa, when the time is right.' My father couldn't believe it! 'What?! are you crazy?' he shouted. 'Why my daughter? She's never even been to Okinawa!'

"My father didn't know, but my mother and I often visited the *yuta,* her friend who lived down the road. She never told my father, because he wouldn't approve of more hocus-pocus. A *yuta*, you know, is a healer, an Okinawan shaman," she explained to me leaning her head even closer to mine as we sat there already like Siamese twins on that loveseat. "*Yuta* give spiritual guidance to people, cast out demons," she paused to make sure I understood. "This is what I learned a few years ago at a lecture at the university." Mrs. Urabe now studied my face. "Do you believe in healers?"

I was willing to believe, because my own grandmother had

healed me when I was a kid, but my asthma wasn't caused by demons. "Well, maybe," I replied.

"*Yuta* are very powerful women, you know, really strong. I must admit at that age I didn't always know what was going on, but I saw people crying, barking like dogs, running around on their hands and feet. We lived in the sugar camp at that time." Mrs. Urabe's lashes fluttered in time with her accelerating words. "*Inu-gami*, dog-spirit possession, some people said. They talked about the power of evil, making people do what they don't want to. She cast out these evil spirits; she smelled smokey." Mrs. Urabe stopped, took a deep breath, looked out into the air and started again.

"The *yuta* went home to Okinawa the year before I got sick. Now the *obôsan* said I was possessed by spirits from Okinawa. When we learned that, my mother and I looked at each other. We were afraid to tell my father about the *yuta*. Even though he didn't believe the explanation, my father expected my fever to go away."

I wanted to take a breath for her; her words tumbled out so fast I thought she might faint. I felt my eyes widen and my stare intensify. She didn't seem to notice.

"After all, we'd gone to the *obôsan*; he prayed for me and explained the problem. We had even offered incense and money. The priest had cured other people. But, I didn't get well. My mother and I knew it was because the *obôsan* was not Okinawan."

This subtle difference escaped me. I wondered why not being Okinawan had made the *obôsan* unable to cure her. After all he was Japanese.

She continued, "Without knowing about the *yuta* my father arrived at the same conclusion. The *obôsan* from Japan had no effect on these Okinawan spirits. 'We need to do something different, we're now in America,' he said.

"So, we went to a small Christian church. My father made us go. It was strange. I had always been curious, but most of the people at the camp went to the temple. Here was a preacher, and he wasn't even Japanese. After my father explained my situation the preacher said he knew demons were causing my fever, and he had the power to cast them out. I was shocked; I didn't know there were demons in the Christian Church. The preacher said we had to be there on Sunday and that I should dress in white. That day he called me to the altar and shouted, 'Lord, Lord, give me the power, the power, to do away with this evil.' His voice rose higher and higher, and the people in church cried out louder and louder. He poured water over my head. My tears started to flow. I heard myself wailing, 'Lord, Lord, make me whole.' The fever left me. And we became members of this church.

"Several years later I understood why I had been possessed and why I needed to become Christian. God wanted me to cast out demons myself. He had given me this experience so that I could use it for others."

I wanted to ask why she needed to be a Christian, why being a *yuta* or an *obôsan* wouldn't have sufficed but didn't want to interrupt her line of thought or ask her what might have led to theological considerations, so I sat quiet, my wheels turning.

"That experience gave me first hand understanding of the torment of demons, you see. Today some call it depression, bipolar condition, schizophrenia. Labels don't mean anything to me, because all demons somehow respond to the Lord. The Lord Jesus Christ found me so that I could cast out demons."

She looked at me. Our eyes met. She smiled just like in those images of Jesus you see on Christmas cards. I should have been reassured, but somehow I began to feel uneasy.

"The Bible talks about falling into fire and water. I believe that describes an epileptic fit. Lenny, another one I helped, was in an auto accident and lost consciousness. The Bible says, 'Demons like to go into empty houses.' That's when they entered him—in the hospital—when he was unconscious. It was like he was clean, clean of thoughts, clean of wishes, desires, knowledge. Becoming possessed is a result of becoming clean; there's a vacuum that needs to be filled. Before the accident he loved Japanese ghost stories and myths. His room was full of *tengu*, you know those demons with long noses. After becoming possessed, Lenny did unspeakable things. He said there was a craving in his bones. I'll never forget those words. I won't tell you exactly what he did. You really don't want to know."

"No, please go on," I pleaded, "I'm curious."

"You know what they say about curiosity. No, it will only make you sick. Then, you'll be afraid, you'll be afraid. Francis killed a marine, when he was seventeen years old. No one knew why."

Francis? What happened to Lenny? I wondered.

"Just out of the blue, he killed him. I read it in the paper and wanted to see his parents. I prayed about them for five days, and a mutual friend brought me to them. The mother showed me her shelf lined with images of different gods. Christ on the cross, Christ standing, okay, but there were Buddhas sitting, Buddhas standing and Shiva, Vishnu, Ganesh, Guanyin, you name it."

Mrs. Urabe turned to me and said, "You don't have images of gods in your house, do you?" She looked right through me. I shook my head no, trying to erase the image of my collection of Buddhas.

"God says, 'I am a jealous god.' 'You have too many gods.' That's what I tell them, when I point to the shelf of idols. Francis' father hits the table and says, 'That's it, we don't have the real god.' I agreed with him and said, 'But you do have Christ here. Keep his image; get rid of the others.'" She looked at me in a knowing way.

"They let me visit him in prison. He was wild, wild, so wild. His eyes didn't look straight; they moved from side to side as if he was looking at something moving in the room. He let me pray for him; his mother just cried and cried. Then I started seeing red marks on his arms. They got redder and redder. He started screaming, 'Stop, stop, don't hurt me.' Those red marks became teeth marks right before my eyes. Then they started to bleed. I opened the Bible to Luke 9:1 and read, 'He called his twelve disciples together, and gave them power and authority over all devils, and to cure diseases.' 'That goes for us, too,' I told Francis, 'we can cure, we have authority over all devils. We have the power, the power.' His arm stopped bleeding before the guard came back.

"It took me months of prayer to make him better, but, you know, I never told him to be good, as in good good, because if you're too good, the Devil will want you."

I felt dizzy. Lenny . . . Francis . . . I needed some air.

"Mrs. Urabe, what do you mean, good good? You're a Christian. Aren't Christians supposed to be good? As good as can be?"

"Yes, yes, but not good good. Too much perfection, and you compete with God," she said with some finality, beads of sweat appearing on her upper lip. She looked at me, "Well,

I've told you only some of my stories; I have a lot more to tell. Now would you like to be my writer?" she asked. "You are a good listener."

The Ant Massacre

"I don't know what's wrong. Some keys seem to be stuck," she said leading us to the far corner of her living room. A dried out Christmas tree stood next to the Hamilton upright. It was March.

The piano tuner lifted his eyebrows and frowned.

"Have you been seeing any ants lately?" he asked acting like Mike Hammer.

"How did you know?" she replied her voice rising.

"Well, Christmas trees and plants around the piano is a no-no," he answered pointing at the dried up poinsettia on the piano. "You shouldn't put any plants near a piano. Attracts ants."

"Really?! No one ever told me that. I'm so sorry," she answered her voice getting softer.

"He's not scolding you," I added for reassurance, "just letting you know." Clients sometimes misinterpret my husband's bald statements. Really, he's just giving them information not condemnation.

"When ants find a cozy place where they're not disturbed, they make a nest. Making a nest means gumming up the place. Their bodies produce a very sticky substance. You'll probably see some today. It will be everywhere inside your piano," he warned.

Mildred moved away from the piano.

As if to confirm this analysis a few ants came up from between the keys, flaring their antennae before they slithered back in between. The piano tuner tinkled a few keys; a few more ants came up for a look. "We'll need the vacuum."

"OK, I know," I said, heading for the door.

By the time I had returned from the car with the portable vacuum cleaner, the piano tuner had removed the keyslip and the sideboards that held it in place. "Where's the nearest outlet?" I asked holding the electric plug in my hand.

"Behind the Christmas tree," Mildred answered. She had been standing there, helpless.

I groaned inside and crawled behind the tree. Each time I nudged it, a shower of needles cascaded on me. "Sorry about the mess," I apologized trying to leave the irony out of my voice.

"Don't worry," Mildred replied, ignorant of the omission. "I should have gotten rid of it months ago."

Emerging from behind the tree, I shook my head and rained needles.

In the mean time the tuner was about to remove the middle keys. "Ready?" he asked. Yes, I nodded holding the long, hungry nozzle above the keys. He lifted five keys with one thrust of his fingers. As he did so, they came frothing out—black and white, frenzied bodies carrying white sacs in their mandibles. To save the colony, no doubt. From previous ant hunts, we guessed that the sacs were baby ants. The white membranes shaped like minuscule peanuts were carried like precious cargo. Nothing could be seen inside. But there was no time to examine the contents. At first they scurried in every direction, bumping into each other. They were leaderless. Frantic.

Because of their size these carpenter ants looked fierce, a moving canopy of warriors. As more and more piano keys were lifted, hundreds of agitated bodies overflowed from hidden places into exposed spaces. The wiggling bodies went in all directions. Only a few seconds later they seemed to be following some signal and moved in one direction. This made it easier to suck them up with the vacuum. A fever of emotion. I whipped into action, fanning the nozzle across the keys, sucking up as many mad ants as possible. I moved it back and forth, up and down, into the exposed crevices, swooped over moving black and white dots from one end of the key bed to the other.

"Don't move," I warned my husband and sucked up some errant ants climbing up his arm.

The nozzle passed swiftly over darting bodies. No escape. Sucked up into oblivion, reduced to debris in the dust of other old pianos in the vacuum bag, I thought.

"Watch, watch, watch," I uttered in staccato beat, falling to my knees now, moving the nozzle along the trail of ants heading down the piano leg. The piano tuner jumped out of the way.

Mildred just stood there, frozen, as she watched all these unwanted guests scooped up. "I didn't know, I didn't know," she repeated. "How did they get here?"

"They were born here," the piano tuner explained, pointing his screwdriver at the piano. "Do you play the piano?" he asked, placing the last of the keys on the floor beyond the tree.

"No, no one plays. It was my daughter's piano, but she's away at school. She came back for Christmas but didn't play. Didn't have time and said it was out of tune. So I thought I'd have it tuned, just in case she came home on a visit. But, no, no one plays," she said in stilted syllables.

"Perfect incubator. The piano is perfect, warm and cozy because of the damp chaser. And if no one plays, it's quiet. They've been multiplying here all this time. A perfect ant condo," he repeated.

"Happy, happy and safe. That's what they were," I jumped in. "Not so happy now," I added. "Good thing they're not marabunta," I chuckled.

"What?" Mildred queried, coming out of her daze.

"What are you talking about?" my husband asked, a slight irritation in his voice.

"You remember, don't you? The marabunta, the marabunta, from the movie, *The Naked Jungle*. There were millions and millions of swarming ants. They looked like a moving carpet. They ate humans. Good thing, these aren't marabunta."

The piano tuner gave his driver a dirty look.

You Eat at the Old Gibson's?

"Assagios? Dragon Court? Gold Coin?" The woman named all the restaurants where she had worked, trying to pinpoint where she had seen the piano tuner. "I know I've seen you somewhere, wish I could remember." She walked ahead of us as we picked our way through the sundry pairs of slippers, shoes and odd toys strewn in the hallway. "Yeah, I think I've seen you before." She didn't mention me, didn't even look in my direction. Why was it so important to know where—if—she had seen him? She set her head askew and bit her lip as if still searching her memory.

"But, I know you, don't I?" she badgered, lingering on the *know*. She looked straight through me at him. After a moment, "You eat at the old Gibson's?"

"What? No," the tuner answered curtly, irritated by her persistence. "Where's the piano?"

"Right over there," she pointed toward the far side of the room, "Go straight through to the other room." She paused for a second, "Sometimes?"

The tuner ignored her question and proceeded to the piano. I wondered whether he had gone somewhere without my knowing and was trying to hide the fact.

The Chinese character for luck in red hung upside down in the hallway. I was tempted to point it out to her, but figuring the client to be Chinese, I assumed she knew better than I. I stared at the upside down character in passing and wondered at its mystery almost knocking down some boxes of dolls and games lining the end of the hall. It was a long hallway.

Her daughter, Crystal, I learned, was in the sixth grade, though looking like a ninth grader. She sat on the floor with Andrew, her younger brother.

"He's ADHD but higher functioning," the mother explained. Andrew did not look up. "He can do almost anything Crystal can, but I have to keep an eye on him. He's very active. Aren't you, Andrew?"

He looked up at her, narrowing his eyes and wrinkling his nose at her. "Why do you have to tell everybody, Mama? She doesn't know me," he protested, quickly pointing his nose at me, then looked down at his favorite X-man, Wolverine.

I really didn't want to get involved in the discussion, so I smiled and headed for a chair.

"Now, Andrew, be nice. ADHD is nothing to be ashamed of. You need to integrate. You know, I've been going to those special workshops for you between my jobs. I want you to do good, baby. Be happy." She smiled at me in complicity and squatted next to Andrew. She touched his head as if caressing a cat. He wiggled away. She sat there, cloyingly attentive. "You know, Mommy loves you and Crystal very much. There's nothing she wouldn't do for you. Happy, I want you to be happy. Remember what I said about finding pleasure in all kinds of things? Little things." She paused, "Then you won't get frustrated." Crystal gave a side glance to her brother, who nudged her with his Wolverine.

The children continued playing with the mother hovering over them. "I want you both to do real good in school. You know, Mommy never got to go to college, but you will because you're going to study real hard and make Mommy and Daddy proud. Aren't you?"

"Did you really want to go to college, Mom?" Andrew asked, moving Wolverine's arms around.

"Yes, I did. I was going to go to the community college, but then Crystal came."

"Yes, you told us that before, Mom. Then, I came. But you never explained why we came. Couldn't we have waited till after college?" Andrew asked.

"You and Crystal couldn't wait. You wanted to come, so you came."

"Couldn't you make us wait?" he pressed.

Loud, staccato hammerings came from the piano as the tuner checked on the spring mechanism. Everyone looked toward the piano. Then the mother continued, "No, Andrew, children don't wait, they come, when they come."

"Couldn't you go to college anyway?" Andrew pressed.

"No," she replied emphatically, looking directly into his eyes. "I had to work and take care of you and Crystal." She ruffled up his hair again and gave him a smile. Turning toward me she said, "It's hard to explain to children, isn't it?" I nodded yes.

"You know, Mommy, you can go to college now, if you kill us," Andrew said in a matter-of-fact tone.

Home Sweet Home

Upon entering the living room I was drawn to a huge aquarium occupying half the wall opposite the entryway. A big moray eel coiled in the lower corner of the tank moved its mouth in rhythm with its undulating body, a sultry hula. Our eyes locked. I wondered whether he'd been fed. A small yellow tang high above him twirled its pectoral fins warily. Better him than me, I thought. On the adjacent wall sat a fifty-two inch flat screen showing what looked like a National Geographic program on the ocean. More creatures of the deep. An octopus slid across in high definition. No sound.

Turning from one scene to the other, I said to no one in particular, "This is amazing."

"It's my hobby," a voice offered from nowhere.

I looked behind me, and stretched on the sofa in the middle of the room was a young man ear phones on head. I wondered how he could have heard my comment and how I could have missed his presence. "Hi," I said trying to camouflage my surprise. He nodded his head sliding back into the fold of the sofa.

Mrs. Tavares returned from the kitchen carrying a tray of drinks. "My son," she said tilting her head in his direction. "Can't find a job," she clucked. "Let's sit down here." She indicated a love seat beyond the sofa on the other side of the huge room.

"Too bad," I offered as I followed her. She lay down the tray on the table in front of me. "Thanks for the treats."

"He's married, but he lives here at home." Her voice, flat, matter-of-fact, she looked in his direction, while taking her seat next to me. "You don't mind, do you?" she asked and continued, "His father-in-law doesn't want him touching his daughter." She didn't notice my eyebrows rising, her eyes now looking down toward her lap.

"Mommm," the son pleaded from his side of the room. "You don't have to tell everyone, you know." I see hands adjusting earphones.

His hearing is so fine, I marveled to myself and wondered what I had gotten into.

"Young people today," she said, shaking her head, her eyes trained on the tray. "How did I raise him this way! Girlfriend *hapai*. Gets married. Stays home." It seemed all a mystery to her.

I remained completely silent fiddling with my book. I really did not want to probe, especially with her son eavesdropping. I hoped that the piano tuner would start punching the notes loudly enough to stop the conversation.

But before I could be saved, she asked, "What do you think, missus?" raising her chin and looking at me.

Taken aback, I stammered, "Think? Oh, I don't know, don't have a son, no children. I guess we saved ourselves a lot of grief," I chuckled, looking toward him. His head had not emerged from behind the sofa, though I was pretty certain that he could hear our conversation.

"Oh, I'm sorry. Don't get many visitors, you know. My husband is at work and my son, well, as you can see, he's real busy." She tilted her head slightly in his direction. "I finished all my housework this morning, and my TV is broken," she confessed.

I turned around to see that the flat screen was off. Her son must have left the room.

"I keep on asking myself, what did I do wrong? A son marries, he should live with his wife, no? Isn't that the way it's supposed to be, missus?"

I nodded in agreement, but before I could say anything, she continued. "Now, why would a father refuse to have his son-in-law live with his daughter? After all, they're married. He did the right thing. They had a nice wedding. She's going to have a baby. Happy ending, right? Anyway, what right has the father-in-law to say, no! She could come here and live with us. We have plenty of room."

Taking another sip of water, I nodded again in agreement, but just as I was about to ask a question, she added, "On the wedding day, before they're supposed to go to the bridal suite, the father tells us, 'Okay, from now on you live separate.' We were so shocked, we didn't know what to answer. By the time we understood what he meant, they left. Gone. We all went to the bridal suite to talk it over. My son was confused; he thought that the problem was solved. My husband wanted to punch out the father, but what could he do? His son made his daughter *hapai*. That night we decided to let the father have his way, we felt so bad. In any case, my son prefers to live with us. No one bugging him about getting a job or helping around the house. Just me. He doesn't hear me any more.

She paused. I had nothing to say. Nothing to ask.

Why the Boxes?

You asked, 'Why the boxes?' OK, why the boxes. I'll try to explain. I want to tell you everything, because I don't want to be unfair, you know, just give you my point of view. But then everything gets kinda mixed up. Sometimes I remember wrong. How do I know it's wrong? It feels wrong. My body doesn't feel right when I tell it. But I've told it so many ways. To the police, to the firemen, to my son, to my neighbors and now you. You doubtful? You understand what I mean, don't you? OK.

See, there was this fire, and the house burned down, no, not my house mind you, my neighbor's. Because he didn't call the fire station, the fire came to my house. I know, I know, stupid, yeah. So, my kitchen burned. Now you see why the boxes. I know, it's awful. You look like you understand. Look at all these boxes. I've been living from boxes for over a year, ever since the insurance people sent the packers here to salvage what was left. My kitchen was gone. Totally. The roof just caved in on everything. Too bad my office was connected to the kitchen and all my papers—all my papers—got soaked. Thirty years of tax returns. All my papers. Good thing the piano didn't get wet. I need it. I need to play. Thank goodness your husband agreed to tune it. I need to play, really, I need to play.

You see, next door, that new house. They broke down what was left of the old one. Nothing, really, just cinder blocks, black, left standing. They found him dead, you know, in the bathtub. I guess he thought the water would save him. He forgot about the smoke. Why didn't he just get out of the house? He had time.

They found a few empty fire extinguishers lying on the floor. One in the bedroom, another in the bathroom, where he was in the water, dead. Sad, yeah. You're right, it was awful.

I was watching MacNeil Lehrer—I know that's not the name now because one of them must be dead, but I can't remember which one—when my son rushes into the room and asks me whether I smell the smoke coming from the neighbor's yard next to my kitchen.

Thank God, I didn't die; I didn't even get burned. The piano didn't get wet. I count my blessings. Everybody tells me to count my blessings, and I do. My piano was saved. Most of my house was saved. Every day I tell myself, I must count. I didn't die. And I could have died. But look at this mess now. All my belongings in boxes. My papers matted together. How can I find anything? I've lost a whole year out of my life because of that fire, and nothing's back to normal yet. Why didn't he call 911? Why did he wait until he died, and it was too late. All he had to do was run outside. Yell. Say something. But no, quiet until the end. Always quiet. Never yelled, never fought so that you could hear. No. No.

I bet you know people like that, never say a thing, never complain, and then something happens. Say, that's a nice necklace you're wearing. I used to like necklaces, but I've stopped wearing them. Calls attention to my neck. Look at this turkey neck. Terrible, yeah. Try pulling your skin like this. Ever worry about getting old? Avoid it. What am I saying! The only way to avoid it, is to die young. Now, I don't mind people looking at my hands, then they'll see my diamond ring. Makes me remember my husband. Pretty big, no?

Yeah, he had a chance to call 911, but why didn't he? My house wouldn't have been damaged, if he called them right away, but no, he tried to put out the fire himself. And then he crawls into the bathtub and dies. My daughter down the street called. So did other people. No one could give the address; it confused the firemen. They went down another cul-de-sac, and that's why my kitchen roof caved in. Now I'm living out of boxes. I can't even find my coffee mugs. How do they expect my life to get back to normal.

I know, you want to ask me why I don't unpack . . . Oh! I see you're looking at the boat in my garage. That's my husband's. I'm supposed to get rid of it; just haven't gotten around to it. Have his rifle collection, too. Now all rusted, no one to take care of it. His clothes, too. He died 20 years ago. I know I should get rid of it, everyone used to tell me I should. Never got around to it. He died when they tried to reshape his heart. I told myself, I'd give it time. Now I have to deal with all these boxes. Is it normal to live out of boxes? In your own home?

I ask you, why didn't he call 911? The houses are so close, you can hear if anyone raises their voices. But no, the only way you know someone is home is if you look in the carport. I guess he tried to put the fire out by himself, but he couldn't do it. When the firemen investigated they found the extinguisher, "spent" they said in the report.

He was always a quiet man, him and his wife. Really nice people. But you know what they found in his house, well, I don't know exactly, because I didn't really want to ask, but I heard that he had piles and piles of junk mail all around. Oh, his wife died years ago and his children, they live on the mainland. So he lived here alone. His house was full of old junk mail from the 80's, junk mail. Imagine that!

Pete's House

I remembered Pete's house from when I was a kid, going to Manoa Elementary School. It was across the street from my sister's piano teacher. It was the best looking house the Woodlawn bus drove past. I knew it was Pete's house because I saw him get off the bus and run up the lawn. He was in my class.

Even if I never went inside, I imagined that it was like the haole houses in front of ours. I got to see inside, because my sisters and I played with the haole kids. Their house was big, lots of room. High ceilings with more than one living room. They used to have the tallest Christmas trees I ever saw, right in every living room. Maid's quarters. Most of the houses around where I lived on Woodlawn except for the two front houses were Japanese houses. Somebody told me the restrictions against Asians were lifted at the time my parents bought the land, and Japanese families came in. You could always tell which houses were built afterwards.

Sure, ours was big; we had ten people living in it, but our front neighbors had no kids, and the other family had three kids, only five lived there. But both houses were much bigger than ours.

Ours was a simple, single-walled construction built by my father and uncles and other carpenter friends. Raw concrete floors downstairs, unpainted hollow tile. The Fosters had this lush, white carpet, a color my mother would never have chosen. That's where I learned haole houses were different.

The bus stop was right in front of Pete's house, and I'd

watch him run up that perfect lawn to an open lanai. You could sit on these lounge chairs and probably see who got off the bus. Or admire the pink and purple impatiens lining the flowerbeds overflowing with red roses, hibiscus and lilies. It all was so elegant and genteel.

Today I got to see inside Pete's house, not just the outside. No, Pete doesn't live there any more; now the Chuns do. And we tuned their piano. When she called, the piano tuner told me where we were going. I didn't know that it would be Pete's house. I only knew the bus route and the curve in the road.

To get to the door we had to walk on some cut up carpet pieces laid out on the wet lawn like stones. At least there wasn't any mud. No impatiens either or roses or any flowers whatever. Just weeds. The lanai was crowded with stacked up lawn chairs, all kinds, white plastic cape cod chairs, folding chairs with canvas seats, high back sand chairs. Some folded up and leaning against the wall.

Outside the front door toaster ovens were stacked up. Westbends, Westinghouse, even a Cuisinart. Two-slicers, four-slicers. But none of them work, Mrs. Chun later told us. She said Mr. Chun picks them up at garage sales, off the street, anywhere he sees them. Most only need a new latch or a new thermostat. He's going to fix them up and sell them. He's been collecting them for twenty years, since he retired. He hasn't sold any yet. But he's started on the repair, you can see toasters in pieces on the dining room table.

His son found six miniature copper barrels of yeasts and oats sitting on the side of a road. He's going to make designer beers. The barrels are stacked up three on top of each other on the inside of the hall wall. He hasn't started yet because he hasn't found any kegging equipment at any garage sales. He's sure that he soon will. Without this equipment it would be silly to buy the hops or any of the other supplies for the beer. In any case, he hasn't found a book with directions either.

I noticed boxes full of kewpie dolls, hair spiked out from the plastic scalps piled along the floor next to stacks of yellowing newspapers and magazines. The dolls are hers, she explained. She just likes to collect them, and they are getting rarer and rarer. All this, Mrs. Chun, explained as she led me and the tuner through the maze.

"They're named after Cupid, you know, the Roman god? God of beauty and non-Platonic love. What do you suppose that is?" she asked, not waiting for an answer. "Just ignore the mess. We've learned to live with it."

It really wasn't as bad as what you see on *Clean House* or *Hoarders*, at least there was space to move, at least there was a plan, a reason to keep it all.

As for the newspapers, she didn't explain.

How Soon We Forget

"I just want to let you know that next week, when I see you again, I won't remember you, your name, your face," she said, as she brushed some hair away from her eyes. We had just gone through the routine pleasantries and the initial evaluation of her piano. It would require a pitch raising today and another tuning next week. So we left the tuner in the back room where he was inserting the red felt tape between strings. Then she showed me to her living room. "Here you can see the lights dancing off the water. It's really pleasant," she said pointing to the ocean outside her picture window. In the background, you could hear the quick bounce off middle C.

It was then that she hit me with that most startling statement. "I won't remember you."

I didn't know what to reply. What are you supposed to say? "No need to apologize, I have a forgettable face." As she continued explaining other facets of her forgetfulness, I was drawn to the memory of an old college friend. Yeah, Patti and I had been inseparable buddies in school, but a few years later at Safeway, I think, she didn't even turn around, when I called out her name. I wondered, did she hear me? We hadn't parted on good terms, but shouldn't she have said hello? Maybe it wasn't her. These thoughts rumbled through my head along with the irritation at having been reminded of them. Thankfully, Marsha Collin's voice cut through my thoughts, "I have this condition, you know, it makes me forget even before I have a chance to remember."

Having just read Oliver Sacks, I shook off my own thoughts and wondered if she suffered like the man who mistook his wife for a hat. His memory loss was profound. He had to be introduced to his wife every time she visited him at the hospital.

"It's not all the time, for everything," she added breaking my reverie, "just once in a while. And, no, it's not the beginning of Alzheimer's," she explained anticipating my question. "The doctor says, intermittent memory loss."

She looked me straight in the face as if studying it. I wondered why she bothered. After all, she had just declared she would forget it. "I know we'll have a nice chat. You look like a good listener. You are, aren't you?" she said lifting her eyebrows ever so slightly and turning the ends of her lips into a meek, apologetic smile. Patti had a smile like that, I thought. She'd apologize about everything, even when there was no fault to find. It was only later, that I figured her out.

I wondered if Marsha was like Patti, but Marsha exuded straightforwardness, nothing ironic here. I returned her smile and readied myself for a long, unexpected afternoon. The G above middle C reverberated from the other room as I tried to remember every detail.

To look at her face you would not think, yes, this is a Marsha Collins, military veteran. No, she looked like my mother, nisei, second generation—too Japanese to be a Collins, too old for inter-marriage, too sweet to be a military veteran. A slight woman—local lady—a plain, ordinary lady, my neighbor, maybe yours.

Only thing, she had this uncommon condition, something memorable.

In one avalanche of words she told her story, letting all the details tumble out, no doubt, for fear she'd forget something. At age thirty-eight she had epilepsy, a condition that had not appeared earlier. What a coincidence! That's what Patti suffered from, except hers was from childhood, controlled by medication. I remember we got close after one of her episodes. She had forgotten her pills. She asked me to keep her secret. Poor thing, she didn't want anyone to know. Patti was more afflicted by her own fear that others knew than by her condition. Marsha seemed not to share that fear. Moreover for someone who wasn't going to remember the piano tuner's wife next week, she seemed to have full command of the details of her life, which for some reason she wanted me to know.

During her monologue her eyes focused elsewhere, her lids twitched from time to time, and the lines around her lips quivered. "You see, I left home real early, because my parents were dead, and my aunty and uncle couldn't really afford to raise me. They had enough children of their own." She paused as if counting them and sighed deeply. "I met my husband in Germany, where I was stationed in the fifties. Typing was mostly what I did. My husband was a sergeant, you see. He'd come into the office and chat. He's dead now, but I have our sons," she paused, picked up the cushion next to her. "Have to sew this tear," she mused showing me a break in the fabric. "How do you suppose that happened?" I looked at the cushion not caring to answer. "When I lost my husband last year, I panicked. He took care of everything, had to. He reminded me of what I had forgotten, what I needed to remember, mostly people. I remember how to cook, how to drive, how to clean the house. It's faces I forget, you know, new people, like you."

Finally, the main question that was buzzing in my head was answered. I nodded and felt the muscles around my eyes tighten and thought better of interrupting her. "New people," that's what Patti had said, "You should date new people, not the boyfriend of your best friend." I tried to concentrate on Marsha's fascinating tale, but Patti kept on interfering. I pushed her out and listened.

"I was frightened; who would take care of me? None of my sons would live with me, I didn't want them to, no, I didn't," she raised her voice. Noticing my look of alarm, she softened her voice and changed her pace. "I decided to look for a church. There must be some reason for all this, I thought. The nearest one to my house is the Assembly of God, you know, the one on the corner." She turned her body to point in a direction that told me nothing. "But I resisted, no, not there, I told myself, crazy people, you know, anyway that's what I heard." She looked at me and wiped her lips with her handkerchief.

I squirmed a little.

"I didn't want to go, but he told me to go, God told me to go, he did, he did. So I went. I knew there was a reason, a reason for everything, so I wanted the Lord to use me, to use my body, my soul, my mouth, my everything." She spoke faster and faster.

Her unexpected agitation alarmed me, and I found myself clutching the sofa.

"I felt compelled to go to that church. I was being pulled, yanked across the threshold to the altar. No one was there, but I felt this urge to kneel before the cross. That's when God told me I was the most ungrateful wretch." She started to slow down continuing her conversation with God.

"'What have I got to be grateful for?' I demanded.

'How did you get here?' He asked.

'I walked?' I answered.

'What did you walk on?'

'My two legs.'

'Are they strong?'

'Yes, but they're fat and ugly.'

'See what I mean? Ungrateful wretch.'"

She spoke as if from a pulpit, full of fire and conviction. Then her voice calmed, and she gave the smile full of innocence.

Why was she telling me all this, I wondered. Does she know something about me? Am I an ungrateful wretch? The story seemed to have a profound though confusing lesson. I had been so angry at Patti, at her ingratitude. Yes, I went out with her boyfriend one time, not a date, but to talk about Patti. She had gone home that weekend, and he needed to talk to someone. I didn't tell him anything. But a while later they broke up, and I guess she thought I had told him about her condition. I hadn't! That snub irked me. She should have remembered me; she should have remembered all the times I backed her up.

"I'm sorry, I didn't mean to upset you," Marsha said. "I get carried away. That experience was so meaningful to me. I like to share it."

"Upset me? I'm not upset," I blurted, shaken out of my recollection. "I appreciate your story. Why would I be upset?"

"I don't know, you just looked kind of funny. I know I was going on and on. I'm sorry." Her apology drifted into the air.

Feeling rather awkward, I tried to make things right, "Oh, really, I'm not upset, just thinking about something I can't forget."

Maybe Yes, Maybe No

When asked a question he only laughed an answer or cocked a head. Since childhood he had never been encouraged to articulate an answer, let alone be quick or witty or expressive. Too many words put together too well were only signs of a devious nature. And everyone knew that he was open, frank, and honest.

At least that's the explanation I made up for myself as I listened to the piano tuner's conversation or lack of conversation with Cyrus. After opening the door for us, Harold, his brother, left to do some errands, leaving Cyrus in charge. That's what he told him, "Cyrus, you understand now, you're in charge, so keep watch," Harold said, giving a wink to the piano tuner.

Cyrus was so curious about the piano that he peered into the open action to examine all the hammers and strings on the bass side. It was a console model, so he could see everything without being in the way. His head bobbed from side to side as he watched the tuner's every move, and a slender line of saliva shined from the corners of his mouth. From time to time he'd crane his neck so that he could see where the tuner's hand had plunged between the strings and action to retrieve an object that had fallen there.

"Is this your pencil?" the tuner asked, lifting the object out from behind the action. "You know it's not good to leave things like this on the piano. They can fall right inside."

Cyrus listened, but he didn't answer.

"Are you the one who plays the piano?" the tuner asked as he examined the bushings under the keys.

"Maybe yes, maybe no," Cyrus answered.

"Do you like the piano?"

"Maybe yes, maybe no."

"Funny answer," the tuner said, striking middle C. "Don't you know?"

"Maybe yes, maybe no."

Now Cyrus didn't move, just stood there, watching. Clients, especially children of clients, often like to watch. They've never seen the inside of the piano. Sometimes, they lean over and touch the strings, bang the keys, ask questions. Cyrus wasn't at all disruptive, you could almost call him sweet. Though he seemed not to know his own mind, Cyrus just stood there and watched; he knew he was in charge.

Raymond Loves to Talk

Raymond sits there, his ring finger cutting the air as he tells the story about his son in Bhagdad, calling every day about Snoopy, the dog, waiting at home, waiting, waiting, for the return of Popsy, his son, from Bhagdad.

He has a grand piano as well as an upright; that is to say, his daughter whose family lives in an addition upstairs has an upright. The grand sits in the downstairs living room; the upright, in the upstairs living room. They're all there one cozy family, one generation literally above the other. His upstairs daughter is a dentist, his son in Bhagdad, a lawyer, another daughter, a physicist, lives in San Diego with her "partner." He says "partner" with no explanation.

Raymond's quite content with what life has brought him and more interested in the troubles he sees around him. He tells about the ex-senator who's not going to be elected US senator because the merchants in Chinatown removed his placards, after they read about his wife inheriting money from a man for whom she was the caregiver. No, she wasn't doing it now, not after she married the ex-senator, but while she needed to work. Her client was alienated from his son who did not live in Hawai'i and gave her his money. Everyone in the Chinese community believed that she should have relinquished her claim to the family inheritance, after all she was not family, even though she had treated her client as family more than the son.

Blood is thicker than water, much thicker.

He tantalizes me with these stories, moving his eyes this way and that, while the pleasure of telling every detail seduces me to silence.

With no need for encouragement he moves on to the story of the haole milkman who married the Chinese piano teacher. Her mother, brothers and sisters, all refused to go to the wedding. The milkman invites the aunties and mother-in-law on a trip to the west coast. There they discover he's a millionaire with land in Nevada and oil in Oklahoma.

Also, there was the girl who thought she had hit the jackpot when she married a prince who had a home in Mumbai. Set up for life, she thought, servants, jewels, parties, the whole shebang, until she got there and found out that she was wife number three, later to be replaced by numbers four and five. She ended up mopping the floors of the palace.

Raymond loves to talk.

Dog Food Container

A chain link fence surrounds the houses, arranged not one in back of the other, but two next to each other and a third set back. I look for the lever to open the gate, and just as the gate grinds open a monstrous German Shepherd appears bounding from behind one of the houses, barking. Quickly I close the gate and wait. "Did she tell you about a dog?"

"No. Here, boy, come." The piano tuner leans towards the fence and extends his hand to the dog.

"Don't do that!" I shout. By the time the words are out of my mouth. The dog is licking his hand.

"We can go in," he assures me. The dog's tail is swishing back and forth, and his tongue is now licking the tuner's face. "He likes me," he says, crouched before the monster.

"I can see that, but don't let him do that!" I scold. "You don't know where his tongue has been."

"Hi, I see you've made friends with Smooch," a woman coming from behind the house yells out. "He ran out of the house before I could stop him. He barks but never bites," she assures us extending her hand to the piano tuner. "I'm Gladys."

"He's a monster. I mean, he's huge," I comment.

"Oh, yes, he can go through quite a few bags of Pedigree a month.

"Pedigree?"

"That's his dog food," she replies.

The piano tuner has been tagging along, listening to our conversation and explains, "This is my wife."

Gladys nods her head as if an explanation was unnecessary.

She swings the screen door open and leads us to the end of a dark hallway, where the piano is pushed under the stairway ensconced in its niche.

"It's dark here, but perfect for the piano. When I play, I don't bother anybody, and it sounds good here. After all this time my brother wants to play his ukulele along with my piano. So we need to tune this. There's some stuck keys, too." She caresses the finish of the piano. "I know," she pauses, "doesn't look too promising. Looks like burned alligator skin. Can I do anything about that? At least it still plays, until now anyway. Like I said, the sound is nice and rich under this stairway, like in a chamber. I think it's a Knight. Have you ever heard of that make? Somebody told me it was expensive."

"Yeah, Knights are all right. Made in England, you know," the tuner says.

"Really? It came all the way from there?"

"They started selling them here in the 60s, I think. Yours doesn't look like it's had much upkeep."

I cringe at that comment and want to give the tuner a nudge, but he's too far away.

"I'm sorry about that," Gladys apologizes, "you know how it is. The piano's the last thing we spend money on."

"Oh, he's not criticizing, just making an observation," I assure her.

Gladys continues, "It's been working all right, mostly. As long as I can get a sound, it's fine. But now the pedals don't even move." Lifting the fall panel that covers the keys, she pounds on a few, "You see, the middle C is sluggish, and the A above won't even work. You think you can fix it? How much will it cost?"

"I can't tell yet, just give me a few minutes. You say the pedals don't move?" he asks while pushing his right foot on the soft pedal. "No soft pedal."

"See what I told you? So what would it cost?" Gladys asks again.

"Did you know, most people don't use the pedals," the piano tuner explains, while removing the panel below the keys. As he lifts the panel, reddish brown, nugget-sized things tumble out from the bottom of the piano.

"What is that?" I ask.

"Don't know," the piano tuner replies.

We go down on our hands and knees to examine what looks like dirt colored pebbles. I lift one between my fingers and sniff. I hand it to the tuner who is already examining his own pebble. We look at each other and turn to Gladys who is looking down at us. "What did you find?" she asks.

"Come look," the tuner replies.

Gladys goes down on her hands and knees, too. "What is it?" She takes one in her hand, "What the . . . Pedigree nuggets? How many?"

"Bags full," I reply.

"The pedals couldn't move because of this stuff all around the mechanism," he says as he pushes a wave of nuggets from out of the hollow of the piano.

"How do you suppose that got there?" we ask each other.

Morocco

We could have made a down payment on a condo with Harrison's piano.

Every week or two the piano tuner would be called to replace broken strings at the Morocco nightclub. It wouldn't be just one string but at least two or three, sometimes more. Thank goodness it was a grand piano whose open guts lets you work the strings with less hassle than uprights. It's not enclosed. It's exposed. To hell with spinets, so manini with their space, so secretive like a girl holding her legs together. Replacing strings on an eight-foot Baldwin still isn't easy money, but it's not as great a headache. At $75 a string, more for the copper-wound ones, and $90 for the tuning, the tuner could easily make a few hundred with each call. Maybe not as much as an electrician or a plumber but better than a schoolteacher.

"How does Harrison do it?" the tuner muttered as he leaned into the belly of the grand. "Week after week broken strings. This piano's not that old."

"Maybe it's the ocean; we're not that far from the beach," I offered as I leaned over into the guts.

"The strings really aren't rusted. Take a look," the tuner said pointing at the break in the string. "Still shiny. In fact, I think I just replaced this one the other month. Shouldn't break like this. This is the highest gauge steel core, coiled with thick copper. Broken," he said, shaking the broken string in his hand.

I shook my head, too. Then he said, "Never mind, it's good, real good. Now if you'd only stop buying dangling earrings, we might put together some real change," he continued with a teasing grin.

"When did I buy dangling earrings?" I muttered.

Why would they break week after week? Even newly replaced ones? Since we hadn't had a date in a long time, we decided to make a night of it.

Our reservation was for eight so we arrived a little later. At about a quarter after, we entered a room full of people, sitting on elevated platforms, padded with cushions. During the day the room looked empty, which seemed strange. Now it made sense; the arrangement delighted. We were in an exotic hideaway, barely lit, with the scent of cloves wafting from a *houka*. We ordered what the waiter suggested, some kind of lamb and eggplant and, of course, couscous. The double martinis put us in a very good mood. This was not like our usual outing to Zippy's.

Dinner finished and the second martini taking effect, I smiled at the tuner and floated above the cushions. Harrison took the stage. Enthusiastic applause. I joined in by slapping my hands on the table, not too smart since it shook the martini glasses. Dressed in a black tuxedo with glimmering black lapels, hair slicked back, Harrison sparkled, no, he dazzled. His patent leather shoes shimmered.

"For all you ladies," he said and started to sing in a honey voice, "She can kill with a smile . . . she can lead you to love . . . she's always a woman to me . . ." The piano tuner glanced at me, humming along, "she never gives in, she just changes her mind." Billy Joel, Harrison, no, it was the martini. I rubbed my leg against the tuner's.

Taking an unexpected turn Billy Joel became Ray Charles, singing to Georgia in the most soulful way. This was most surprising, unexpected. The voice! The emotion. However good the show was, nothing yet explained the broken strings. Soulful, mellow. The mystery remained. We discussed this, the piano tuner and I.

Harrison wailed another song, "He'll trade the world for the good thing he's found." The piano turner was transfixed on a half-clothed waitress returning with his third martini. "If she's bad, he can't see it, she can do no wrong." The piano added the throbs of the heart. Perturbed, I pinched the piano tuner's arm.

"What'd I do?" said his widened eyes.

Harrison changed the pace and became more and more agitated as he dove into, "You shake my nerves and you rattle my brain, Too much love drives a man insane." The audience bounced on their cushions. Several couples got up and started to dance. Harrison gyrated crushing the keys with his two octave hammers, his hair up in the air, his legs pumping up and down to the percussive bumps and the jet stream glissandos. At the climax he lifted his left leg and punched the bass notes of the grand piano with the heel of his foot still covered with his shimmering shoe. We heard a copper string snap like a whip with metal tips. We looked at each other and smiled.

Soon after that we read in the paper that the Morocco had been sold to a developer. A condo now sits at that spot, condos we could never afford.

Brat

"Hello, Old Lady," the child says to me her eyes looking right into mine. Stunned I push the ends of my mouth into a smile.

"Now, Lindsey, is that the way to say hello?" the mother says smiling at her precious one. I feel my mouth tensing into a smirk.

The child turns to me and twists her lips and peers at me through the exaggerated narrowness of her smiling eyes, "I'm sorry."

"What can you do with kids today?" the mother continues with a shrug not looking at her daughter. But I know she thinks her darling is cute, so clever, the brat.

I look down at her, but her mother is there—as is the piano tuner—so I give her a special smile. She smiles, too, that one.

"The piano is in the other room. Over here," the mother says directing us away from her child. That one stands by the wall with her little rag doll, head hanging by two threads, grinning.

Before she can come out with another "old lady," I follow the mother and tuner into the living room. She is enjoying her upper hand . . . I wince. Then a poem by Raymond Queneau comes to mind:

> If you think, sweetie pie
> if you think, yes, yes
> your pink cheeks
> your honey bee waist

your cute little biceps
. . . if you think sweetie pie
it's gonna, gonna, gonna
last forever...
but the good days fly by like
the beautiful party days. . .*

I smile to myself, though I feel her eyes piercing my back, her lips no doubt widening on that small face. My throat feels dry.

Sitting in the room across from the piano I look at the crook in my arm and stare at the play of skin. I pinch it and lift up some flesh. It does not snap back as I remember it used to. My only consolation, I know that young thing has no clue how fast the good days fly.

*Raymond QUENEAU (1903–1976)
L'instant fatal (1948) Translated by Jean Toyama

The Inheritance

As you move past the picket fence, you can see that the perimeter of the yard on the right and left is lined with papaya trees. One lime tree peeks out from behind the left hand corner of the house. A tall mango tree shades the house from the front. It's only one story high, like most of the houses on this street, nothing fancy with space for kids, space for trees. Mrs. Grace is a long time client, one of our first. Always kind, always hospitable.

"Here, try some of my cookies. They used to call them Russian cannonballs, but the young people today call them . . . what is it, they call them?" Mrs. Grace pauses. "Sweet melts, that's it, sweet melts. I suppose, that's a better name. They do melt in your mouth." As she places the platter of sugar dusted delectables in front of me, the aroma of butter fills my mouth, and I can almost taste them. Mrs. Grace sits down beside me.

"Oh, Mrs. Grace, you spoil me! I gain weight every time my husband comes to tune your piano, but never mind, I've loved Russian cannon balls since Stevenson Intermediate time." I stuff my mouth full. "Those cafeteria ladies sure knew how to make them. Just like you," I say exhaling a puff of powdered sugar. "Excuse me!"

Mrs. Grace gives a laugh as she hands me a napkin. "You like them, huh?" she smiles. "My husband never ate any. Too sweet, he would say. But, you know, I made hundreds, no, thousands. Sometimes every inch of this room would be covered with cakes, pies, cookies. Have I told you this, before?"

she asks reaching for another melt. Not stopping a beat, she continues, "My favorite was carrot cake. It sold real fast and I made good money from that one. Grew the carrots out in the back." She jerks her head towards the kitchen as she licks her finger tips. "No, Herbert, didn't like sweets. Of course, he had diabetes, so it wasn't good for him. That's why I could bake so much. Good thing! Don't get me wrong, I wasn't happy he had diabetes, but this way he couldn't eat the profits. Practically paid for this house. He died last year, you know, just after your husband tuned the piano. I remember the piano was in good shape, when the family came over for the wake. We sang all his favorite songs."

Mrs. Grace speaks with a gentle lilt like many older Portuguese women, though she was only part Portuguese being a mixture of Hawaiian and Chinese. She wore her heritage well, each playing a part in her manner. Her husband was mostly Hawaiian the rest being an indistinguishable mix of east and west, English, Irish, German, Japanese, Korean. They had five children, four girls and one boy. Four were still alive, the oldest daughter, the beauty Julie, having died of cancer long before her father.

"You know, a few months before he died, he tells me he wants to leave the house to Herbert, Junior, our son. I asked him what about Hannah and Emily, they're not married. Eleanor has her husband to take care of her. Sorry, to unload on you, but you know, it still bothers me. He tells me, oh, they'll get married, their husbands will buy them a house. I didn't want to be cruel, but I reminded him that it was my sweets that paid for the house, that I should have a say. He didn't even want us to buy the land when we got married! Can you believe that? 'We don't have the money, we don't have the money,' he kept on saying.

"Anyways, my two bachelor daughters are almost fifty. What was he thinking, my husband? Do girls get married after fifty? Didn't I have a say about who would get the house?

"When my daughter-in-law heard about what her father-in-law said, she started plans for renovations. Now, don't get me wrong, I like her. She's a good girl," she said, jutting her jaw out, exploding each syllable. "But, the nerve, I wasn't even dead!" After a pause, "Good thing Herbert never like to deal with details. We only had a deed, Herbert and me, 'tenancy by the entirety.' That's what the lawyer called it. Now I get to decide."

Tiger Knots

"We can do it. I know we can do it."

"Stupid, that's an old wives' tale, a custom, not even mine. Anyway were in the 21st century. Give it up! You're Japanese, not me. You believe, not me."

I was eager to hear the conversation floating out from the room next. Yes, I'm an eavesdropper. I had nothing to do but wait for the piano tuner, and I heard these voices.

I glanced through the open door. The women talking were not visible, but the voices were strong and sharp.

"That doesn't matter. We're a melting pot, remember? We both eat sushi and pork adobo. It don't matter. Like I told you on the phone, we can make one."

"You don't know how to make one. You don't even know what it's called. So how are you going to tell me how to do it?"

"We're going to do it. We're buddies. Get it? We'll take the one I have apart and figure it out."

By this time I was straining to hear, trying not to miss a word. I heard a distant ping and thought the piano must be way off somewhere. I had a delicious feeling coming over me, listening to a conversation not meant for my ears, trying to figure out what they were talking about.

"I tell you, this will work. I know it looks awful. It stinks, but if we take it apart and study it, we'll be able to make a pattern from it."

I strained to see the speakers. So engrossed were they that I could have been sitting next to them, and they would not have noticed. The reluctant one, sitting on the sofa with her feet up on the coffee table, crossed her arms around her chest. The persuader was holding something in her hand that looked like a rag.

"It was in my mom's closet. After she died, we cleaned up the house. Looks like something I should have thrown away, yeah? But see, it's got these red knots. At first I thought Turk's head knot, you know, one of those complicated round things with threads going in and out, but look."

The persuader clucked her tongue and leaned over to offer her friend a look at the old dirty rag.

"Funny, it doesn't smell," the reluctant one said, "it looks like it should smell old and musty."

"The knots are simple. We can do it," the persuader continued. "French knots, all in rows."

At first I didn't know what it was. Then I remembered my mom telling me about how she followed her mother around asking people to sew knots, when her brother was going off to war. He came home alive and well and *baban* told everyone it was the power of this thing that saved him. That's what my mom told me, anyway.

The voice paused, "He came back from war, alive!"

I waited for more talking, instead I heard the piano tuner running his fingers over the keys. No doubt, to see how stuck they were. That's what had initiated the trouble call, stuck keys.

"You think it will work? You think Ryan will come back alive, if . . ." Her voice trailed off, and the insistent pounding of the piano keys masked whatever emotion I imagined. "How will we make it?"

"Like I said, we can pull this one apart."

"No need!" the other exclaimed, "We can google it."

"Google what? What's its name? What will you google?"

I wanted to run in and tell them, "No need, I know, I know, it's a *sennenbari*. It means a thousand needles." But then, they'd know that I had been eavesdropping. So I moved away from my perch out of visual and listening contact. I knew how to make one of those protective belts. No doubt, they could follow the thread of the key word and come upon instructions on Google, if they knew the word. But how would you know, *senninbari*, if you didn't know it? What could you look up in Google?

My uncle was going off to Korea. I was only in the fourth grade, but we understood that he was going to war. Twenty-one, no wife, no children, fresh fodder for war. That's the kind the government likes, young, unattached . . . green. There was no question that he wouldn't go. No one protested. They just went. But before he left, while he was in training at Schofield, my grandmother had us all sew red knots into a long piece of white linen. She had marked off straight lines in light pencil.

But she was special, her *senninbari* would have more power. She was doing it for her son, but she was also a tiger and knew her own power. She could sew more than the one knot ordinary women were allowed to sew. She sewed more. She even plucked strands of hair from her head and twisted them into the thread. She must have thought her hair powerful. Now that I think of it, my grandmother was very inventive, she took something she learned and made it her own. She let me sew as any many as she did and used hair from my brush to tie in with my thread.

No doubt I believed. Was it the thousand knots or the power of my grandmother? It didn't matter, we were doing something for my uncle who was going away. Can a nine-year-old fathom death? Maybe. My five-year-old cousin had died that year. We knew we wouldn't see her again. We are such puny creatures, but sometimes with iron faith we think that our small action can stop bullets. You think too much, I told myself. Why not the bliss of indifference? Why not the belief that there is nothing to be done. Then you could be done with it.

I got up from my seat and I started for the room where the women sat talking.

"Excuse me, is there a bathroom I could use? Oh, what is that you got? It looks just like something my grandmother once made . . ."

Story Teller

"Do you think pineapples can grow in Paris?"

What??? I thought. Where did that come from? Here I was, where I didn't want to be, and this guy is asking me a stupid question. "I dunno," I reply. "They grow here."

"Yeah, but we're in Hawai'i. The tropics. There's winters in Paris; it snows. Anyway this guy, Balzac, thought he'd get rich growing pineapples on the hills of Montmartre." He pointed at the book I was holding. "He wrote that book."

I stared at the cover of the book I had just lifted off his coffee table.

"Picked it up at that annual sale, you know the one, Friends of the Library. *Eugenie Grandet* by Honoré de Balzac, it said, staring at me from the table, like I was supposed to read it. Recognized the unusual name from a book I was reading about pineapples. Had to buy it. Who would try to grow pineapples in Paris? Of course, he lost money."

He eased his frame into the rattan chair across from me gently wiggling his *okole* between the cushions. The reeds gave a sinking squeak. I was about to say, "I've read Balzac . . . ," but before I could, he added, "Here, have some coke and *arare*, real crisp, just opened the package." He stretched the bowl out to me and without forgetting the thread of his conversation asked, "Have you ever tried to grow pineapple?" He threw a few crisp rice chips into his mouth and between crunches said, "Takes a long time," he swallowed and stretching his tongue across his top teeth, added, "Do you know Balzac? What a nut! Even so, it's a great read."

By this time I had given up trying to tell him about my own admiration for Balzac, perhaps the most famous French novelist of the nineteenth century, and asked instead, "So did you find out what makes him tick?"

"The verb to have. It's all about having. Grandet wanted to have. Money, land, orchards, oh yeah, and gold. Even so he lived like a pauper. So it wasn't what money could buy but just the having. Every morning he counted the sugar cubes to keep track. Didn't want anyone taking more than allotted. I think Balzac himself wanted to have, too." He pointed his teaching finger at me, "But I guess he wanted to have something else, like the pleasure of writing stories or accumuating stories; he wrote so many. Anyway, that's what the intro says."

While he took a sip of coke, I marveled at Haruo's insight, "Yeah, I never thought that you could have stories." I wanted to tell him about my own efforts to write but thought better of it. I remembered with relish Monsieur Grandet's mole quivering every time he cut a canny deal, like the time he made believe he was losing money on land, when actually he was chiseling his neighbor. In any case, my host had already returned to the kitchen where the icemaker gave a crackle. He was in and out, here and there ever since we had arrived to tune his piano.

Upon returning he asked, "I did tell you my name, didn't I?" pointing his index finger to his nose, the way the Japanese do. "Hal Haruo Holden." He lingered on the Haruo, looking at me with anticipation. After a pause he continued, "I bet you're wondering why I have a Japanese middle name. Everyone asks why," he chuckled. "Pure haole . . . with a Japanese middle name. That's because Mrs. Inoue gave it to me," he announced proudly. She was his landlady from long ago who had a heck of a time saying, Hal. Sometimes it sounded like 'hell' or 'hairu.' Finally, she christened him Haruo, as in 'son of spring.' "I just love that idea of being spring in Japanese. Can you imagine me going to school with a name like Spring? Yeah, I'll never forget that gift," his voice drifted; his belly jiggled gently.

Since the piano tuner was busy in the other room, doing his work, I was left being entertained by this client. After Balzac's pineapples I was given his life story including his stint in the Navy and three marriages. His latest, and I assumed last, was to a young "local girl", Harue,—just a coincidence—who added two boys to a varied crew of children from his other spouses. Haruo and Harue, if not born of the same season, blossomed together.

"You know, before I married Harue, the pastor called me in and asked if this time, I was sure. He had officiated the other two weddings. Well, I must have been." His hands opened wide in a welcome. "We've been together over twenty years." His voice rounded softly; his eyelids relaxed for a second. "Too bad, she's not here for you to meet. You'd see why I'm such a lucky guy." He shook his head as if agreeing with himself.

Now that's something a Japanese husband wouldn't say out loud, I thought.

"By the way how are your feet? Ever get any pains under your arches?"

I was taken aback by this strange question. "Well, once in a while I have a sharp pain, but it goes away after I massage my feet." I could feel my brow tighten. "I think it's plantar fasciitis."

"Well, maybe. But see here, I've got lots of really satisfied clients who've bought these special slippers. Let me show you."

He leaned over stretching his arm around the sofa and produced a pair of blue bedroom slippers. "Magnets, that's what it is, there's magnets embedded in these soles." Lifting the pair with one hand, he pointed at the soles. "You can't even feel them, but they'll soothe away any ache." He stretched his arm towards me. "Here, try them. They're Harue's. Looks like you both wear the same size."

"Really, no, I don't have much pain," I said, raising my palms up. "Like I said, goes away after a massage. I thought you sold insurance?"

He seemed not to hear and, bending over, placed the slippers right by my feet. "Yeah, I do. But since I've got the clients, I thought I might as well tell them about these great slippers. I tell them stories, while they try them on. Slippers and stories, they go together, don't you think? Old people suffer from sore feet. Stories distract them."

Slippers and stories? That's a new one.

Haruo kept on, "I'm not saying you're old, but old people, they never get relief. The doctors give them a song and dance, telling them it's part of getting old. Live with it. Can you believe that? Relieve pain. That's what I think they should do." He paused and looked at my feet. "I heard about these magnet slippers and tried them out. They worked for me, so I make them available. Don't make money off them," he added.

"How do they feel?"

"I was . . . I was just wondering, do they really work?"

"If you don't have any pain, you know they're working. Doesn't that make sense? Go ahead, walk around. Harue won't mind."

I couldn't argue with him. He's the kind of guy who tells you everything on his mind to make you laugh or convince you he's telling the truth. In other words, you can't say no, so I walked around, did knee bends and tiptoed around the coffee table. That day I left with a new pair of slippers, the cost of which was deducted from the piano tuner's fee.

After bringing out a new pair of slippers he said out of the blue, "I bet you're interested in astronomy. You have that twinkle in your eye." I blushed. "Too bad it's not dark, I'd show you my telescope in the back yard. Built it myself with the help of my friend from Mauna Kea. He's an engineer at one of those telescopes. Mine's not bad for a small one." By this time I was convinced that I had encountered the uncommon here on an aging sofa. "It's so powerful you can see cepheid stars, you know the pulsating kind, that that guy Hubble used to measure starry spaces." I tried to give a knowing look. Hubble, the telescope? I wondered.

"You know, Hubble, the astronomer who figured out distances in space," he explained, no doubt having interpreted my blank look. "It just amazes me that when I look through my telescope, I'm looking back into time. Doesn't that boggle your mind?" he asked turning toward the bay window that framed his own little Mount Palomar. "The light from the big bang is everywhere, because everywhere is the result of the big bang. What a miracle it all is!" he sighed.

Balzac and pineapples. Slippers and stories. Why not the Big Bang? After all, writing stories is like looking through time and space.

While the tuner worked on Haruo's piano, I learned that he used to be a bus driver in Waipahu, a Fuller Brush man in Honolulu, a vitamin salesman and a butcher in Nanakuli. Only after twenty years has he found a steady profession, selling insurance, no doubt while regaling his clients with stories.

69

"You know O. camp, no? The one down the road. Used to be part of the plantation. It's now a one hundred-fifty acre piece. Heard about it?"

"No, can't say I have," I replied.

"City girl, huh? Well, Mr. O—don't want to tell you his real name—was a crafty Japanese entrepreneur. He knew how to chisel the land out of the hands of four friends. He never told them that the plantation had offered to sell the land they were leasing to grow pineapple. He knew English better than any of them, that sly fox. So, Mr. O. acted like the head of the group and got the land for himself."

I listened as he expressed each detail with excitement, his eyes widening and narrowing with intensity, occasionally shining with expectation. He spoke with so much animation, caressing every word, stopping, pondering as he piled one detail on top of the other. I admired his enthusiasm, his ability to let the words tumble out as if they were straining for the moment of birth, pushing against the womb. He had no fear of being rejected or boring anyone. I looked at him with envy.

"Lot's of stories in Hawaii, yeah," I commented.

"You bet. Mr. O. must have had a mole on his nose," Haruo reflected, "and it quivered a lot."

Uncle's

Uncle's was almost empty except for the bartender and two women at the counter. Not unexpected, after all it was only 10 in the morning. But I was surprised that these patrons were already lifting a few. I looked around for a chair and table. I had my choice. The piano was across the room away from the bar which stretched along side the entrance where daylight showed through. Everything else was relatively dark. The place smelled old, old wood, old pine-sol mixed with clorox. The nicked furniture and peeling paint just added to the authentic feel of age. But it was clean, sort of. The tuner had examined the spinet and judged only a simple tuning necessary, which amazed me. Places like this usually need much more done to the piano, since management waits until it is practically falling apart before calling.

The bartender had just uncapped a couple of Michelob light for the women. Neither turned around to look at us; they had the mirror behind the bar to observe. One of the women was a brunette with strawberry accents swimming through her hair cascading way down past her ample *okole* which spilled over the edge of the seat. A yellow hibiscus sat above her right ear. The other one sat in the shadow. "Sit anywhere you like," the bartender shouted from across the room.

"Thanks," I replied taking a table between the piano and the bar. I didn't want to have the sound of the keys pounding in my ears. I looked forward to reading the latest issue of *Sci-*

ence News which I had been carrying around in my book bag along with Murakami's *Kafka on the Shore*. Opening the magazine to the wonders of quantum theory, I felt a presence at my right elbow.

"Wanna beer? the voice asked.

Startled I replied, "A little early for me, thanks." From the top of my glasses I saw a rather attractive woman with a long mesh of hair curled over her shoulder. Her eyelids were perfectly made up, though the blue-green eye shadow took too wide an arc over the edges of her eyes. She gave me a smile and pointed to my magazine and book.

"You, one teacha?" she asked. I nodded yes. "I told you, she one teacha," she shouted to her friend still at the bar. Turning back to me she said, "I can always tell."

"You mean I look like a teacher?" I asked narrowing my eyes.

"Don't you?" she replied, widening hers. "What's wrong with dat, looking like a teacha? Always wanted to be one."

Thinking no answer needed I returned to *Science News*.

"Hey? what's wrong, why don't you answer?" an indignant voice said.

Startled, I blustered, "Sorry, I'm not being rude; it's just that people always say I look like a teacher. It irritates me, you know, the pigeonhole."

"Let me tell you, I know about pigeonholes," she replied moving her head up and down, her voice less edgy. Her lips turned a sly smile. "They call me Star. You can, too." She extended her hand and said, "My friend at the bar is Bernice." Without moving her head, she yelled, "Say hello, Bernie." Bernice with the cascading hair waved from the bar.

By this time I had a better look at my questioner. She was tall, quite pretty, really. No flower in her hair, just natural;

nonetheless there was something there. Her eyes opened so widely I wondered whether she had had something done. Her face bore few wrinkles, but the skin around her neck folded on to itself. Her Adam's apple protruded suspiciously. Star smiled again with a quick lift of the eyebrows. No botox there.

"Why you stick around your husband so much?" She paused waiting for my answer. "Maybe, you protecting him, because dis one bar?" Star smiled seductively, her lips arched mocking.

"No, nothing like that. It's just that he doesn't drive," I explained.

"He don't drive? Bernie, he don't drive," she yelled.

In the background an echo, "No, I don't drive."

Star turned toward the tuner and commented in wonder, "For real? I thought all men drive."

Not missing a beat as he moved the tuning hammer back and forth, the tuner added, "I can't drive. I'm visually handi-capped."

Surprised, Star walked over to the piano looked closely without being rude and exclaimed, "Blind?" She jerked her chin back. "You don't look blind."

"Star! Leave the piano tuners alone," the bartender barked.

I was happy to be included in the category.

"Yeah, Starry Girl, come back here, I'm getting lonesome," Bernie at the bar added.

"I'm not bothering them," she muttered, brushing her right hand against her hair as she walked back to the bar. "Ber-nie, I thought dat one stereotype, blind piano tuners. Lots of tuners not blind."

"But before time a lot of blind people went to tuning school. Just like my uncle," Bernie nodded, pointing her finger

73

for emphasis. "You know what they say about blind people and hearing," she explained.

As their voices receded I became engrossed in dead and live cats, Schrödinger's cats. This was a thought experiment that preceded the Heisenberg effect. There was a box with a cat, dead and alive, in limbo between the two states. Only when observed would it be either one or the other. It all had to do with perception and reality.

I sat there puzzling over the whole quantum of it, when a voice came, "Sorry, yeah, sometimes I get nosey. He don't mind, yeah?" Star asked, returning this time with her Michelob in hand.

Forced out of my quantum cloud, I babbled, "Don't worry, your questions don't bother him. He can see enough but not enough to drive."

I could feel that Star wanted to continue our conversation and waited for her next comment. "So, is that all you do? Read science magazines?"

I didn't want to try to explain dead and alive cats, so I pointed at Murakami's book, "Sometimes I read fiction."

"Say, *Kafka on the Shore*. I read that last year. You like talking cats?"

Before I could express my surprise, Star turned to my husband and shouted, "Hey, piano tuner, you wanna beer?" She lifted her Michelob and pointed at it.

"No thanks, not now, maybe after I finish. If I drink now, I'm not gonna finish," he chuckled.

She turned to me and said, "Did you notice there's a picture of a weird cat on your magazine? Is that why you're reading Kafka?"

"No," I replied feeling my insides churning. "No, it's just

a coincidence. The article in the magazine is about quantum physics!"

"What's a cat got to do with whatchamacallit, quantum wantum?" she asked reading the cover. "Hey, looks interesting, 'beyond spooky', it says," Star pointed at the cover, "Spooky? funny word for physics, no?"

I didn't want to, couldn't explain the ins and outs of Schrödinger's cats, so I tried to brush it off, "It all has to do with multiverses. You know, more than one universe existing at the same time."

"Sure, I saw that on *Nova*," Star said in a flat voice. "Has to do with one observer, right? A universe is, if someone sees it. So who's to say others don't exist, if there's someone to see them others. After that program, I said to myself 'so God must be looking at everything, so that everything can exist.' Makes sense, no? If nothing exists, it's because nobody looking, but since everything exist, God gotta too? No?"

I was flabbergasted. Star had just explained the anthropic corollary of the idea based on observation. Just then I heard the piano tuner playing his test song. When he does that, I knew he was finished. Halfway through the first phrase, Star broke in, "Hey, he's playing my song!" Quickly running to the piano she joined the tuner with a melodious baritone ending with, "*She's everything that you would adore . . .*"

After the song she asked, "How'd you know, was my song, piano tuner? *Stella by Starlight*."

"That's your name, right, Stella? Star."

Her mouth opened in amazement. She shook her head, "And what your name?"

"You can call me Willie," he replied with a smile.

"And your driver, what's her name?"

"Wife."

Everyone laughed. "For real, what her name?" Bernie asked.

"What's your name, Wife?" the tuner asked as he lifted his bottle toward me.

"You can call me driver," I replied with a grin.

"Whaaat you don't like your name either?" Star snapped.

"No, I just don't like the puns people make with my name, 'Winnie, you one winna?'"

"Better than you one whiner," Star smirked.

I winced.

With all the music and laughter wafting out the door, more people started to come in and fill the tables. By this time, we were well beyond our second Michelob.

"Let's sing something Hawaiian," I suggested. Then I hummed a few bars of a tune that had haunted me.

"Oh, you singing *Kanaka wai wai*,"Bernie chimed. "You go to church?"

"No," I confessed, "but I like the tune. Teach it to me, will you?"

"Willie, you know it?" Star asked.

"Just sing it and I'll follow."

Most of the patrons knew the song, except us. We just followed along with lala's in harmony.

After we had sung it a couple of times, I asked, "What's this song about?"

"As far as I can tell it's about a rich man who had trouble going through the eye of a camel. He no can pass through," someone explained.

"Through the eye of a camel?" I pondered, taking a long swallow of beer. "Now, that's from an alternate universe.

Stillborn Stories

Aproru Pansu

It sits there on top of the glass cabinet in the corner examination room of the Hawi Health Center. It sits there because no one has ever bothered to throw it away. Twice every year, Mrs. T. wipes the glass container, when she dusts, never looking at it or wondering why they keep it. Pickled in formaldehyde, it could be an appendix. The configuration is similar but too thick, a little too long. Perhaps a worm with only one mouth, just a tube within a tube, like the ancient trocaphore. If you had been there seventy years ago, you'd know that it was C.'s penis. The story of how this organ became detached from its owner is simple. It was cut off. The why is a bit more complicated. That year, as in other years, the circus came to town with its weary elephants, scrawny tigers and hairless lions. But every year everyone came from miles around to take another look. For one thing E. K. Fernandez had the best hot dogs. For another the popcorn wasn't bad. C., the original owner of the penis, was there, too, hot dog in one hand, bag of popcorn in the other. He couldn't eat the popcorn without dropping more on the ground than in his mouth. He managed the hot dog, though it spurted its juices on his face as he wandered head up eyes agog between the ferris wheel and the merry-go-round. Sophisticated fairgoers of today would find no thrill here, but then it was enough to amaze.

C. wandered about, swallowed up by his oversized apron pants, called *aproru pansu* by his Japanese cohorts. He had to have the plantation camp seamstress put up the cuffs which still dragged in the dust and fix the front that looked like a oversized bib over his chest. From one of the tool loops on his hip rose an orange ballon on a string.

This was C.'s first circus. He had seen nothing like it in the small town of S., where he came from. Even the smell of stale alligator dung enchanted him to say nothing of the reptiles themselves, imported to awe the country bumpkins. C. was not awed. He was homesick.

From the ferris wheel people peeped into the K. bathhouse. Nothing really could be seen, since steam covered the tiny glass windows, but imaginations ran amok. The family had seven girls. C. loved being on the ferris wheel looking down and around.

He looked into the sky and saw a myriad of stars arching above him. What is up there? he wondered. What worlds beyond? Usually he did not let these thoughts in. But the laughter, the breaking of the monotony, made him think. He smelled the moist sawdust, the elephants, the roasting corn. The light from the bathhouse stood out among the other lights. Even on the ground he had stared in that direction so often that his eyes did not have to search, they were drawn to the two-eyed windows. He started to move. The music started up again and he descended first in tiny jerks, then smoothly to the sound as he turned on the giant wheel, being moved back and forth and up and down by the machine making circles in the sky. It moved as he moved, and his own stars burst forth to the rhythm of the motion.

From his seat he saw nothing through the steamed up window pane, but the faint outline of something emerged through the leaves of a tree just along side the bath house. Some branches jiggled nervously. C.'s breath shortened, so intent was he on their movement. He wanted a keener look and stood up craning his neck from side to side to find the right angle. He craned his body over the side rail and did not notice that his hammer loop was caught on the latch hinge. His gondola started swinging back and forth as C. and balloon bobbed from side to side. The agitated movement of both gondola and man sent shivers across the rickety wheel. Someone screamed when C.'s popcorn fell below in a magical shower. C. looked straight down and saw space instead of his seat. He found himself now beyond his gondola stretched out half into the air.

It all happened so fast. His pant loop, hooked on to the latch, unhinged the guard rail, and he tumbled down, but not off since he was caught by the pants. He swung helplessly out in the open held securely by the shoulder straps of his apron pants which had neatly hooked onto the gears of the gondola below.

Unfortunately for C., he was not the only thing that dangled out. C. was saved, but his part was not. They took so long to unhook him, the doctor called it asphyxiation even though C. himself had not been strangled in the commotion.

This is why, so they say, a penis sits on top of the glass cabinet in the Hawi dispensary.

Ji Ga Deta

"*Ji ga deta*," he indicated weakly to my grandmother. She responded by reaching towards his rectum and pressing there as if holding in a part that was falling out. In normal circumstances I would have turned away my priggish eyes, but my father was dying. His body in anticipation was falling apart. Bit by bit his strength departed and literally he had to be held together.

He lay there half the body I once knew, the other half having seeped away somewhere, disappeared without our knowledge. It was a kidnapping we couldn't report. Just cancer.

"Hey, you wanna go down to the beach?" asked my cousin. I mumbled a yes and left my grandmother alone with my father in the boathouse. It was a dilapidated wooden structure worn down by many storms, now used only for camping. My father wanted to come back to Kauai just one more time before he died to do what we had been doing every summer on the beach at Maha'ulepu.

The tarpaulin kept the boathouse cool; outside it was scorching. I had to squint; the sun was so bright, but it was good to get out from that dark.

Dying takes so long.

In spite of cancer's sapping the vital forces from each organ, the body functions, however feebly, even on the edge of death. The liver, enlarged, maintains the flow of blood, filters like some torn fishnet letting escape the small but catching the large.

At times my father kept his eyes closed, no strength to even lift the lids, but he was conscious of our comings and goings, complaining when no one was near. Some days his strength returned and he would lift his eyes to check to see who was there. But even his eyes told us there was not much time left. The color almost leeched out completely as if used to feed the cancer. Now pale brown they looked to mark the hours. His eyes used to make us cower.

He slept most of the day, waking only to perform those bodily functions demanded by a recalcitrant corpus that refused to be completely stilled. In bed he held his hands folded on his chest or above his head down on the pillow. One could see distinctly the half right thumb, halved years ago on an automatic saw. It was now more pronounced, more pointed as the flesh around the half gone nail had melted along with most of the flesh of his hand. His hands were mostly joints and bones protruding all the more because of the emaciated wrist. So what as left of the one hundred and fifty pounds? Only a frame, a carpenter's frame which had lifted so many wooden planks off the ground, now only bone and skin, a skeleton so lifeless it could never have housed a robust man.

The body too weak to revolt against death, acted as in truce: no gain, no loss. The postponement of total collapse, of the end, is perhaps the most difficult. To endure the hobbling to the end, the intermittent breaths, the arrival to the final one takes stoicism.

It is this endgame, this refusal of the body to relent, when the spirit has already reconciled itself to it, that is trying. For in spite of one's willingness to die, one's desire to die, the body will not. It makes only small concessions, an enlarged liver today, chills tomorrow, fever the next; but in the meantime it will eat more papaya, pass clearer piss, fart with gusto.

But the inevitable does come. Recuperation is but a false promise, a postponement. The body in one final revolt relishes more food, opens eyes wider, watches television and laughs.

The Japanese call it *nakanaori*, a false healing. The body will not last. This is the way it was with my father. After almost a whole week of eyes sealed shut, he opened them as in recovery, only to use that glance in final good-bye.

Last Gasp

There he is alone, counting the minutes left of his last breaths. Does he know that these are his last breaths. No doubt he knows that it is his last breath because he has been counting them and he knows his quota. They told him his total allotment and then came the last of the lot. His last breaths. He hoped that he could make it half a breath then he would have another half left and then after that instead of the half breath he took a half of a half, a quarter, that meant that he could have another quarter after that, then instead of a quarter breath he took an eighth of a breath, then he had a sixteenth of a breath left. With the sixteenth he tried only a 32nd, then a 64th, then a 128th. By that time he had exhausted his possibilities because his math ability was so limited. But this is all conjecture because what is the difference between half breath and a whole breath, let alone a quarter and 128th of a breath? It was all in his mind. He had thought of the sand and the arrow that might have extended his life because he would never get to the end of his last breath as long as he could keep on cutting the last portion in half. Unfortunately, by the time he got to the last portion he had forgotten where he was and discovered that he had miscalculated and it wasn't his last breath at all. It couldn't have been since he was still alive. So he breathed deeply and long. He had miscalculated. The last breath he thought was the last, must not have been the last because he continued to breathe and he took a deep one and sighed because tomorrow he would have to go through the same thing and his math will not have improved.

You Goin' Get *Yaito*

"You goin' get *yaito*, I tell you, you goin' get *yaito*," snivelled the child, smearing mucous and tears across her face with the back of her hand. With her other hand she pointed her finger accusingly, as if by some terrible power she could light the fire that would smolder on the skin of her tormentor. Mockingly he continued to snap the towel at her hips. It cracked the air with a whack. Though he may have caused those too easy tears, he believed he had not yet done anything to merit *yaito*. To tease the snotty neighbor girl was no offense worthy of that punishment.

Yaito was serious business. He thought he knew what deserved it and what didn't. The time he polished the family's shoes brown might have done it, but he convinced his mother he was trying to do a good deed. The time he tried to flush Duchess, the family cat, down the toilet almost did it. But she jumped out before he could see if she would flush down, so he escaped, too. It was understood that these were playful pranks, not products of malice but of unquenchable curiosity and unbridled exuberance.

Nevertheless, patience was evaporating as the pattern continued. Once, after secretely taking apart the cake mixer, he discarded a few "leftover" pieces. Weeks later the mixer fell apart in his sister's cake batter.

"It's Kazuo again, I know it. Okasan, you gotta do something about him. He's a menace!"

Kazuo was not sure whether people were keeping score. Even the quiet discussions behind his back did not worry him.

After all, "You goin' get *yaito*" held little meaning for him. No one in his memory had ever gotten *yaito*. It was abstract, like "The boggyman will get you."

This all changed when his mother fell ill, and the camp doctors didn't know what was wrong. In desperation his father went to the *ogamu* lady who prayed for people in the camp. She suggested *yaito*. She had a friend in the neighboring town who had learned the ancient art in Japan. It was then that *yaito* became a reality to Kazuo.

She lay there on her abdomen, back uncovered to the crevice of her buttocks. Even though they had bathed together in the bath house, as was the custom, he had never really looked at her body. Now for the first time he was seeing a human being. The last of eight children he was given the privilege to sleep with his mother until the age of six. He sometimes even found comfort in suckling like a baby. Her smell and her warmth always reminded him of those moments. Now she was someone separate from him, someone with a body of her own.

Her faded seersucker housedress, a puckered pattern of flower buds, covered her buttocks and legs. A white towel covered her head to the base of her neck at which point he saw tiny black mounds, the size of pencil erasures, rising out from her flesh. Rows and rows of black mounds. He didn't understand what they were. They couldn't be warts, too big for warts. He was puzzling over the constellation of black dots going down as far as her waist, when he heard the *yaito* lady strike a match.

She had torn off small pieces from a sponge-like material and laid them in neat long rows on a low table beside them. Sitting on the floor to the right of his mother she placed a bit of this, *mogusa*, she called it, on the first black mound at the top row to the left on his mother's back and lit it with a stick of incense. He sat hypnotized as that piece of sponge sucked up the orange glow instead of bolting into flame like paper. It bloated fat red and slowly submerged into black. His mother sucked some air through her front teeth. The only sign of discomfort were beads of sweat that oozed from her upper lip and on her tall nose.

While these balls of *mogusa* burned and died on his mother's back, she did not move. He only heard the air moving between her teeth.

The glow moved from mound to mound, row to row as Kazuo sat hunched over his crossed legs. He realized that the black dots were marks from past treatments, scars from being burned. They told him they wanted him to watch this time, so that he would know what yaito was. Yaito as punishment he could understand. Pain for pain. Pain for trouble. Pain for being bad. But pain for cure he could not figure.

What had she done to merit that, he wondered, remembering the often heard menace, "You goin get yaito." If quantity were indication of seriousness, he could not fathom the extent of his mother's crime.

Old Bone

They found some bones in the sand, an old yellowing femur sticking out in a dune. They passed there so often they wondered how they could have missed it before. It looked old. At first he didn't want to touch it, because certainly it was human. But it looked old, and therefore somehow less human. He pulled at it, and it gave no resistance. The sand around it fell quickly in the hole, and you would never have guessed where it had come from. He lifted it to his nose and then realized how foolish it would be to try to smell something so old. There would be no fleshy smell so he scrutinized the surface, making believe that he had really intended to look at it more closely. There were a few ridges around the ball at the end where the bone fit into the joint. The tendons must have been connected at these ridges. He passed his right hand over the surface.
He half expected it to be smooth and was surprised at all the roughness on the surface, not like coarse sand paper but certainly not like cloth. Upon closer examination he saw holes at the top and bottom, at first he thought that the bone had been broken but the smooth edge of the hole convinced him that they were natural punctures, probably for blood vessels.

He placed the bone against his leg to compare it with his own femur and discovered that it was much longer than his. It must have been, he must have been a tall person. A man or a woman? he had no way of knowing.

"Who do you think he was?"

"What makes you think it was a he?"

"Didn't you see how long it is? As long as my leg bone."

"Yeah, but for a guy you're not that tall, you know."

He didn't answer, looked at the bone and started swinging it into to the air. "Catch!"

He caught her off guard, and she fell into the sand as she lunged to catch the twirling bone.

"You never could catch."

"That wasn't fair; you didn't give me any warning," she said as she brushed the rough surface of whitened bone with her palm. "Do you suppose she was Hawaiian?"

"How do you know he was a woman? Maybe Hawaiian. They say these are old burial grounds. Maybe a battlefield."

"Now you tell me," she said tossing the bone to him. "I don't want any *bachi*. No bad luck for me. You're not supposed to go playing around with Hawaiian bones. That's no respect."

"Oh, so we can play with Japanese bones or Chinese bones or Filipino bones."

"You know that's not what I mean. Bury it. Yeah, put it back where you found it. You're not supposed to disturb the dead."

Seven-Year Memorial

They were looking at her, certainly they were looking. Donna felt her head balloon wide and upward so she turned her head down and averted her eyes as she walked straight ahead. To avoid prying looks she trained her eyes on the fraying carpet lining the middle aisle. She turned abruptly into a middle row on the right side. There were fewer people today than at the funeral. Who but the family would come to the seven-year memorial anyway? Why had she come? she wondered.

Really, I don't mean to cause any problems. I didn't come here, because I wanted to cause any trouble. But, you know, it just wouldn't be right. I couldn't let it go by and make believe I didn't know. After all, I went to all the others, all six of them. You know what I mean. After all, it is her seven-year memorial service, for God's sake. Could I just ignore it? Really. What would people think. Just like I didn't care. What would I think of myself? She was kind to me. When she was sick, who took care of her? It wasn't Keiko, her eldest daughter. You can't ignore something like that. I was there at the funeral. In the front row. I gave *o-senko* after the oldest son. My two children gave incense before all other children, even Keiko's. Could I just ignore it? All those years after her stroke, I took care of her. She came to live with us. I asked her whether she wanted to stay with us or with Keiko. She looked at me in disbelief as if I'd ordered her to live with the devil. I'm close to my mother so I assumed she wanted to be with her daughter. I didn't realize they rarely talked except to fight. No, they didn't even bother to fight. They fought too much, too long ago.

The priest directed, "Will the eldest son and his family come up and give incense now?"

Donna slipped into her shoes ready to stand up. She stopped when she saw a man and a woman with two children stand up in the first row. Donna slouched back into her seat. "So that's what she looks like. The color black suits her."

Sewing

My gynecologist is not a good seamstress. When she sewed me up, the two sides did not match. They bunched together. Now the scar's a mess. But that's the price you pay if you want to live. No cut, no life. That's what she said. I needed a hysterectomy. So she got her neat little scalpel and cut, cut and sewed. But like I said, she's not a good seamstress. It takes a lot of patience and caring to be a good seamstress, but you also need to be fast. You'll never get a job as a seamstress if you just take your time and don't pay attention. You need to press on the pedal and go. Watch your fingers! I wonder if the surgeon needs to watch her fingers. Now, why don't the two parts match? Why is my scar so ugly? Didn't she care? Didn't she pay attention? You need to cut it out now, she said.

Good thing I listened, or the cancer would have grown.

Smoke

I always liked her, and she's such a terrific piano teacher. So, I just ignore the smoke, you know, all that smoke around her, and after my lesson it's everywhere, in my hair, in my clothes. But I ignore it. Now I understand it. If I were her, I'd smoke too. I'd drown myself in smoke. I met her son.

Electric sparks, that's what I thought I saw coming out of his head; only they didn't sparkle. They looked like thin, wavy knives. You know how young people, the punks, wear their hair.

He knew me. 'You're my mom's student, no?' he says.

At first I didn't know what he meant. Mom? Student? I would never have connected him to my piano teacher. But now I know why she smokes. I would smoke too. With or without cigarettes. You know what I mean? I'd be burning up inside.

He's a wildman. Spokes coming out of his head. But it's his hair. Evil. If I ever saw evil. It's him. I mean, all that hair sprung out around his face. And that belly. Beer belly. Typical. You should have seen his girlfriend, too. Classic. Massive blue around her eyes, I guess that's supposed to be eyeshadow.

He just came up to me at Ala Moana Park. I mean I was there looking at some vases at the craft fair, and he comes up behind me and pokes my back. You know my mother, Alice, he says, don't you.

Mind you, I never saw him in my life. Didn't know him from Adam. And that look. I almost ran away. But he touches me and calls me by my name. Scared me. I tell you, he scared me.

I seen you at my Mom's, you go there on Tuesday night. Right? His girlfriend tugs at his arm, smiles full of teeth, and he's still grinning at both of us. But it's not a grin, it's a leer. Then he says, 'You want me, don't you,' and runs his tongue along his upper and lower lip. Disgusting. I almost turn away and run, but I don't want to give him that satisfaction. I narrow my eyes and curl my lips like I think a stern mother would do. I wanted to say something. Really, I usually can come back with the best of them. But, I opened my mouth and said nothing, then I turned around and walked away.

I should have said something, something smart and biting. But I didn't.

At my next lesson I didn't mention anything to my teacher. But I couldn't play; I was afraid he'd walk in at any time. I was stupid to feel like that.

I thought, why mention anything. What good would it do. It's not someone you want to remember. You couldn't just say, I saw your son at the park the other day. What could she say? She never even told me she had a son.

Would you want a son like that? Better he'd never been conceived. If conceived, a miscarriage, abortion, anything. Even death in childbirth. I know I sound harsh. Oh, God will strike me dead, I know I sound bad. But I feel so sorry for my piano teacher. How can she live knowing that her son is a freak, maybe worse.

Yeah, maternal love. Endless love. It's beyond me. If you don't deserve it, you don't get it.

Do you have kids? Three? Wow! You are brave. Today having three children can't be easy. I have another friend who ended up in jail because of her daughter. Yes, I kid you not.

Why do they schedule us like this? I've been here already one hour. Wish I hadn't given up smoking

Not Lived

She sat there thinking of all the lives she could have lived
but didn't, all the chances she could have taken but didn't,
all the lovers spurned, all the tears unshed, and she looked
at her book content in her security. She had outsmarted the
veil of tears, the bridge of dreams over the floating world. She
was safe, securely empanelled in the world built so carefully
around her. No chance taken, no risk run. For each decision
a study of the odds. What were the odds that this man would
lead to disaster, this first date to a broken heart? More than
50%. The odds against success, too great, she declined, refused
to go out. Time passed. The going out brought risks of acci-
dents, cars careening into her, strong-boxes falling from over-
head, dead rabbits at her feet to stumble on. So she never left
her apartment. Called out for food, made purchases through
the internet. Thank god for her inheritance. She could live like
this until she died. Until she died.

The Gambler

My purse flapping behind my back, my ponytail falling out from its sequined scrunch, I hurriedly wheeled my grandmother up a twenty-foot incline to the main room. She was agitated and fretful since our arrival and didn't even want to go up to our room to unpack. No, the six-hour flight had not tired her. At ninety-nine she had more energy than I.

"*Ikoo, ikoo*," she exorted, when we finally reached the entrance of the California Hotel Casino. Let's go. Almost every year for the last fifty or so she had made this pilgrimage to feed the bug-eyed slots. I pushed her forward, closer to the edge of the counter so she could reach the square illuminated button marked push and the slit where she would insert her nickels.

Her legs dangled above the floor.

I wanted to place her purse on her lap and advised, "Spread your legs, Grandma." Without cracking a smile, without turning my way, my ninety-nine-year-old grandmother replied, "Why should I, there's no man around."

Baban, I never knew you until that night.

Chicken Scratch

They used to call handwriting like that, chicken scratch and certainly all those markings along the page looked like the work of sharp claws. My cousin's notebooks—the ones filled every day with great earnestness—were filled with pages and pages of these illegible wanton points and angles. My cousin was schizophrenic. Whether all those who suffer from this condition are subject to this same obsession, I do not know, but she filled page after page with "writing", readable or not.

Her condition started in the last year of high school. It was noted that she had the symptoms of appendicitis. She was sent to the hospital, then to Kekela Psychiatric Ward. I was too young to understand any of it or the import of that hospitalization. In fact, she graduated from Kapaa High School and her condition remained a mystery to all.

Her aches and pains must have mounted, because seven years later she was sent to a psychiatrist who finally gave a name to her condition. We were relieved, someone knew what she had.

Sometimes a sense of panic starts descending over her face. It seems to leave the top of her head, go down to her eyes then her nose. When it gets to her mouth, it looks like she'll scream. Sometimes she does, sometimes she doesn't. I don't like it when she does.

Bloody Easy

To assure some kind of excellence one must have begun early. Mozart was four. The only thing I could do at four was bleed well. Even my breathing wasn't up to par; my eating below average, but my bleeding, well, I excelled at that. With so much practice it was no wonder that I was a superior bleeder. But it's not a spectacular gift. Family worry; people pity.

I don't know where this talent came from. It's natural for me, not something I had to work at. It just happened. A line of blood would stream out of the corner of my eye or my mouth or sometimes from the corner of my right thumb. My left thumb. Any one of my fingernails. Any corner of my body. I couldn't predict. It just happened.

Stopping the bleeding was not easy. To stop it, that was the trick. If the bleeding didn't stop, then, well, I would die, of course. When they first discovered my talent and its danger, they tried to replenish my supply with pints and pints of other people's blood. That was a waste. I kept on bleeding. Then they used artificial blood. That's what stopped it. They couldn't explain.

I was a naturally brilliant bleeder, who became artificially normal and alive.

Acknowlegments

Thank you to Bamboo Ridge Press which has supported my work for over 30 years and to the BR study group members who have read most of these pieces and helped me improve them. Many thanks to my sisters, Peggy Cha and Bette Uyeda, and Ethel Aotani, Jean Oka, Joyce Settle for helping with the proof reading. Thanks to Julie Ushio and Katia and Edward Oliver for commenting on the stories at the various stages of the writing.

A special thanks to my editor, Zachary Oliver, for his faith in my work and to Marie Hara for the countless ways she has encouraged me.

About the author

Jean Yamasaki Toyama was born at Kapiolani Hospital, spent her early years at Queen Kaʻahumanu Elementary School and later graduated from Roosevelt High School. She is a retired professor of French and former Associate Dean of the College of Languages, Linguistics and Literature at the University of Hawaiʻi at Mānoa. Her latest books include *No Choice but to Follow* and *Kelli's Hanauma Friends*. Her poetry recently appeared in *Fifty-Eight Stones* and *Wavelengths* from Savant Press and her short stories in the latest issues of *Bamboo Ridge*.

www.ingramcontent.com/pod-product-compliance
Lightning Source LLC
Chambersburg PA
CBHW071109260626
47162CB00006B/2265